Boris
and the
WORRISOME
WAKIES

by Helen Lester • Illustrated by Lynn Munsinger

Houghton Mifflin Harcourt
BOSTON NEW YORK

"All righty, Boris, the sun's coming up. You know what that means for badgers: bedtime!"
But Boris the badger cub did *not* like to go to bed.

"Do I haaaaave to?" Boris said—
just like every morning.
"Yes," Mama said.

"I don't waaaaant to," Boris said—
just like every morning.
"Too bad," Papa said.

So Boris put on his PJs and grumped into bed. His parents gave him a good-morning kiss, whispered "Have a nice day," and tiptoed away.

Before long, the worrisome wakies began.

"My ear itches!"

"I need more water!"

"My covers came off!"

Mama and Papa whispered,
"Go to sleep, Boris."

And later . . .

"I'm hunnnnngry!"

"I think my PJs are on backwards!"

"I can't find my ice skates!"

Mama and Papa called,
"GO TO SLEEP, BORIS!"

And even later . . .

"If I went to the moon, would you miss me?"

"My cuddle-bunny is hogging the bed!"

"I'm scared of the light!"

Papa and Mama badgered,
"Go to sleep, Boris.
GO TO SLEEP, BORIS!
GO TO SLEEP, BORIS!"

But Boris had the worrisome wakies that day and every day. By nightfall, when it was time to get up for school, he was a very tired badger.

Every evening, Ms. Happysnout greeted her students at the door. "Good night, Mabel. Good night, Hubert. *Buenas noches,* Carlos. Good night, Boris."

The other cubs had each enjoyed a good day's sleep. As Boris shuffled sleepily into the classroom, they chanted,

"Everyone join the chorus!
Here comes snoring Boris.
What does he do? Bore us!
Get it? Get it? Get it?"

But Boris just plopped down at his desk and snored.

Boris *was* a boring cubmate,
all through gym . . .

art . . .

lunch . . .

library . . .

 and even music.

And in Ms. Happysnout's
classroom, Boris was usually
a cubby in a cubby.

Boris's cubmates tried to
make him laugh. "Hey, Boris,
want to hear a baaaaad
baaaaadger joke?"

They tried bothering him.
"Koochie-koo."
Poke—poke—poke.

And Ms. Happysnout, unhappily, tried reasoning with him. "Boris, dear, if you slept at home during the day, I'm sure school would be more enjoyable for you."

But Boris's worrisome wakies continued at home, as did his snoozing at school.

After a while, his cubmates stopped noticing sleeping Boris.
Night after night, it was like he wasn't even there.

Cubs bumped into him,

walked over him,

used him as a wastebasket.

Sometimes even Ms. Happysnout forgot him.
"Good night, Mabel. Good night, Hubert.
Buenas noches, Carlos. Good night, Whoozit."

One early morning, when it was time to go home from school, Boris's cubmates were especially loud.
"Was that a great badgerball game or what!"
"And, wow, Ms. Happysnout's exploding science experiment was awesome!"
"Oooo, Mabel's birthday cupcakes were soooo delicious!"
The cubby in a cubby sat up and stretched.

"What did I miss?" Boris asked.

"Lots!" replied his cubmates.

"Like?"

"Like field day. We all got medals."

"And the class picture."

"The school play. You were a rock."

"And your chance to be Line Leader of the Week.
Nobody could follow you."

"Oh," said Boris. "Hmmm."

Tucked in bed that morning, after Mama and Papa
had wished him a nice day, Boris began
the worrisome wakies as usual.

"My leg hurts!"
"I need a turkey sandwich!"

And . . . not quite as usual.

"I want to do a science experiment."
"Somebody bring me a cupcake."

"I really need a medal."
"May I be the Line Lead—"

"Whoa. Wait. A. Minute."

Science experiment. Cupcake. Field-day medal. Line Leader.

All the wonderful things he had missed—and more.

But why? It had to be the wakies! The worrisome wakies!

"Ah-ha!" yelped Boris. Suddenly he knew what to do.

Boris scratched his itchies,

quenched his thirsties,

and fed his hungries.

He adjusted his PJs,

put away his skates,

and tucked in his cuddle-bunny.

Then he pulled down his window shade
so he couldn't see the scary light.

And with that, Boris banished all of the worrisome wakies for good. He was ready for a peaceful, snoreful sleep that lasted all day long.

The next evening, Boris bounced out of bed and got dressed
for school. As he skipped out the door, his parents could only
scratch their heads in wonder. His surprising silence had kept
them awake all day.

Ms. Happysnout was at the door as usual. "Good night, Mabel.
Good night, Hubert. *Buenas noches,* Carlos. Good night—er—"
Who was this bright-eyed cub? "Are you a new student?"
Ms. Happysnout asked.

"You might say that." Boris turned to his cubmates and winked. "Do you want a hint?"

"Yes, please!" everyone begged.

So Boris faked a humongous yawn.

"IT'S BORIS!" his cubmates cried. They could hardly believe it. This cub looked more awake than anyone they'd ever met.

Boris could hardly believe it either—but he didn't want to miss out on a minute.

Now his cubmates sang a new tune:
"Everyone join the chorus!
Give three cheers for Boris!
Hooray! Hooray! Hooray!
Get it? GOT IT? GOOD!"

From that night on, Boris became the liveliest cub in school.
And every morning, he went home for a good, long sleep.

For my husband, Robin, with whom I joyfully pass
the worrisome wakies baton to our own children
—H.L.

www.hmhco.com

The text of this book was set in ITC Espirit Std and Two Fingers Bodoni.

Library of Congress Cataloging-in-Publication Data
Names: Lester, Helen, author. | Munsinger, Lynn, illustrator.
Title: Boris and the worrisome wakies / written by Helen Lester and illustrated by Lynn Munsinger.
Description: Boston ; New York : Houghton Mifflin Harcourt, [2017]
Summary: Boris has trouble sleeping during the day, which is bedtime for badgers, causing him to fall asleep
at night school and miss such delights as exploding science experiments, funny jokes, and badgerball games.
Identifiers: LCCN 2016000982 | ISBN 9780544640948
Subjects: | CYAC: Bedtime—Fiction. | Sleep—Fiction. | Schools—Fiction. | Badgers—Fiction.
Classification: LCC PZ7.L56285 Bo 2017 | DDC [E]—dc23 LC record available at https://lccn.loc.gov/2016000982

Manufactured in China | SCP 10 9 8 7 6 5 4 3 2 1 | 4500632196